ESTRENO CONTEMPORARY SPANISH PLAYS

General Editor

Phyllis Zatlin
Professor of Spanish
Rutgers, The State University of New Jersey

Advisory Board

Sharon Carnicke
Professor of Theatre and
Associate Dean
University of Southern California

Martha Halsey
Professor of Spanish
The Pennsylvania State University

Sandra Harper
Editor, *Estreno*
Ohio Wesleyan University

Marion Peter Holt
Critic and Translator
New York City

Steven Hunt
Associate Professor of Theatre
Converse College

Felicia Hardison Londré
Curators' Professor of Theatre
University of Missouri – Kansas City
American Theatre Fellow

Christopher Mack
Writer and Director
Paris

Grant McKernie
Professor of Theatre
University of Oregon

ESTRENO Collection of Contemporary Spanish Plays

General Editor: Phyllis Zatlin

A SAINTLY SCENT OF AMBER

CONCHA ROMERO

A SAINTLY SCENT OF AMBER

(*Un olor a ámbar*)

Translated from the Spanish
by
Karen Leahy

ESTRENO Plays
New Brunswick, New Jersey
2005

ESTRENO Contemporary Spanish Plays 28
General Editor: Phyllis Zatlin
Department of Spanish & Portuguese
Faculty of Arts & Sciences
Rutgers, The State University of New Jersey
105 George Street
New Brunswick, New Jersey 08901-1414 USA

Library of Congress Cataloging in Publication Data
Romero, Concha, 1945-
  A Saintly Scent of Amber
  Bibliography:
  Contents: A Saintly Scent of Amber.
Translation of : Un olor a ámbar.
  1. Romero, Concha, 1945-
     Translation, English.
I. Leahy, Karen. II. Title.
Library of Congress Control No.: 2005928913
ISBN: 1-888463-20-1 / 978-1-888463-20-0

© 2005 Copyright by ESTRENO
Original play © Concha Romero: Un olor a ámbar, 1983.
Translation © Karen Leahy, 2005.

All rights reserved.
No part of this publication may be reproduced or transmitted in any form or by any means, electronic or mechanical, including photocopy, recording, or any information storage or retrieval system now known or to be invented, without permission in writing from the publishers, except by a reviewer who wishes to quote brief passages in connection with a review written for inclusion in a magazine, newspaper, or broadcast.

Published with support from
Program for Cultural Cooperation
Between Spain's Ministry of Education, Culture and Sports and
United States Universities

Cover: Jeffrey Eads

ABOUT THE PLAYWRIGHT

Born in Seville in 1945, Concha (Concepción) Romero has been motivated by a life-long passion for classical languages, history, cinema, and theatre. While she was completing her degree in Classical Languages at the University of Salamanca, she was also studying Acting in Madrid's School of Cinematography, as well as participating in several theatre groups. Today, Romero is a teacher of Latin and Greek, a screenwriter, and an accomplished playwright.

Romero's theatre is unabashedly gynocentric. Through her unblinking feminine perspective, the dramatist focuses on the female condition and the vital experiences common to women throughout the centuries as they struggle for justice, recognition and validation in a male-dominated society. Her women characters come from all walks of life: renaissance queens and princesses, saints, and nuns, resurrected from obscurity and historical misrepresentation, who clamor for their rightful place in history. Or modern-day divorcées, actresses, and working women rescued from anonymity and indifference. Discreet, clever and witty, her revisionist theatre challenges traditional Spanish conventions and beliefs as it vindicates women's censured role in history, debunks false and persistent myths, and allows an authentic female voice to reverberate clearly and distinctly among women and men.

For the most part, Romero's plays are realistic, psychological dramas that interlace several metatheatrical techniques, like role-playing and the play within a play, in order to unravel female stereotypes and reveal the complexities of human nature. Whether they are our female neighbors, friends or relatives, or Queen Isabella, her daughter Joanna the Mad or Saint Teresa of Avila, the dramatist brings these strong and rebellious characters to life as they battle to take control of their own destinies. If necessary, they are willing to sacrifice everything—love, homeland and profession—for the inalienable right to their bodies, integrity and mind. These female characters do not encounter easy solutions. Victory oftentimes eludes them, and their success can be measured mainly in terms of personal satisfaction. Although ranging in a wide-array of themes and situations, all of Romero's works are characterized by linguistic bravura, clarity and depth.

Romero's theatre surges from two fonts: history and the present. At the helm of the first group of historical plays is *Un olor a ámbar* (*A Saintly Scent of Amber*, 1983), followed by *Las bodas de una princesa* (The Princess's Wedding, 1988), *Así aman las diosas* (This is How Goddesses Love, 1991), *Juego de reinas o Razón de Estado* (Queens' Games, 1991) and *El tiempo de Dios* (Time of God, 1992). The second group of plays is based on contemporary situations and themes that examine the dynamics of modern couples, their falling in and out of love, and the differing attitudes of men and women toward marriage and fidelity. This group includes two ironic and humorous monologues, *¿Tengo razón o no?* (*Am I Right or Not?*, Trans. Patricia W. O'Connor, 1994), *Allá él* (*His Loss, My Gain*, Trans. Patricia W. O'Connor, 1994) and *Un maldito beso* (*A Kiss for a Kiss*, Trans. John Zdziarski, 1989).

Iride Lamartina-Lens
Pace University

CONCHA ROMERO
Photo by Marisa González

Un olor a ámbar, dir. Teresa Sánchez. Theatre company of the Autonomous University of Madrid, performing at the Madrid Ateneo, 1989. Photo by Chicho, courtesy of Centro de Documentación Teatral.

Un olor a ámbar (*A Saintly Scent of Amber*), dir. Teresa Sánchez. Ateneo de Madrid, 1989. Photo by Chicho, courtesy of Centro de Documentación Teatral.

Un olor de ámbar (A Saintly Scent of Amber). Alba de Tormes, 2002. Dir. by Miguel Nieto. Photo by Foto-Estudio Sierra, courtesy of Concha Romero.

Un olor de ámbar (*A Saintly Scent of Amber*). Performed in the Basílica de Santa Teresa, Alba de Tormes (Salamanca), 2002. A cast of twenty, playing the roles of the nuns and monks, was supplemented by an additional twenty representing the townspeople. Dir. by Miguel Nieto. Photo by Foto-Estudio Sierra, courtesy of Concha Romero.

A NOTE ON THE PLAY

During my years at a Catholic high school, I prayed to St. Lucy Filippini. The sisters told us girls of the many miracles St. Lucy had performed throughout her life, but one that I more recently discovered deals with a miracle that took place after she died.

The story goes that 120 years after Lucy's death, her body was exhumed and found "incorrupt": in a state of non-decay without embalming or any mummification. Even the hyacinths in her coffin were reported to be as fresh and fragrant as the day she was buried. That very aroma tipped people off to her sanctity and an investigation into her blessedness began. Nearly two centuries after her burial, Lucy Filippini was canonized.

While Saint Lucy may have a special place in my personal memory, she simply does not rank on the Catholic Saint A-list with Teresa of Ávila. The Spanish Carmelite nun holds her place among Thomas Aquinas, Francis of Assisi and even Peter. Teresa of Ávila is a household-name saint. The author of many books (all available at Amazon.com) and the subject of the Italian sculptor Gianlorenzo Bernini's glorious *Ecstasy of St. Teresa*, she was a mystic believer with an unusually stringent faith.

Concha Romero's 1983 play, *Un olor a ámbar*, grapples with the passionate devotion of the Spanish faithful and the dogma surrounding St. Teresa's relics. A strong subplot underscores the gender battle between the Prioress of the convent of Discalced Carmelite sisters in Alba de Tormes and the Provincial and his monks from Ávila.

It is June of 1583, and a strong scent of amber has permeated the convent since the burial of Teresa of Ávila in October of the previous year. As with St. Lucy, the scent signals that Teresa could be blessed and her body, incorrupt; each finger, a holy relic, quickly gains the attention of the previously disinterested monks, who order the body be exhumed. As suspected, Teresa's corpse is incorrupt.

For many, Romero's play is based on a true story from the sixteenth century. Through Karen Leahy's approachable English translation, Romero's deft exposure of the absurdity and sexism within the confines

Un olor de ámbar (*A Saintly Scent of Amber*). Alba de Tormes, 2002.
Dir. by Miguel Nieto. Antonia González in the role of the Prioress.
Photo by Foto-Estudio Sierra, courtesy of Concha Romero.

of sixteenth-century Catholicism remains, well, incorrupt. In *A Saintly Scent of Amber*, the town of Alba de Tormes and the greater Spanish community flock to the deceased saint's body like a hoard of teenage groupies to Justin Timberlake's backstage door.

Alleged miracles such as that of St. Teresa have been abundant within the history of the Catholic Church. Often, a strange but pleasant scent emanates from the body of a holy person after death. This scent can linger for literally hundreds of years. Amber is not often noted as a holy substance, but the ancient Greeks referred to it as "the holy stone" and used it as incense. Other ancients believed that the smoke from amber could relax and strenthen the body and cleanse the mind.

There have been many cases of oils oozing from the bodies of the blessed deceased. This "Manna Oil of Saints" can cure ills both spiritual and physical. In the play, Teresa's body and her garments profusely exude such oil: Sister Catalina says to the Prioress, "I have wrapped her slip in a sheet and the sheet is now seeped in the same oil. I have changed the sheet three or four times and they, too, have become drenched. It is as if this substance never runs out."

"Relic" comes from the Latin "reliquiae," which literally means "remains." The remains of holy people are kept and venerated for decades, centuries, or even millennia. This adoration is not a uniquely Catholic tradition, however. Relics of the prophet Mohammed, including one of his teeth, his beard, and two footprints, are kept in the Topkapi Palace in Istanbul; bones and hair of Confucius have been preserved since 195 B.C.

Despite any aversion to religious dogma, there are some inarguable truths about the woman Teresa Sanchez Cepeda y Ahumada. Born in Ávila, Spain in 1515 (a contemporary of William Shakespeare), this remarkable woman was fiercely devout, independent and influential. She radically reformed the Carmelite order of the Catholic Church and, at age 47, founded the convent of the Discalced Carmelite Nuns of the Primitive Rule of Saint Joseph of Ávila and continued on to found 17 other convents throughout her lifetime. In 1622, she was canonized, and in 1970, became the first woman to be decreed a Doctor of the Church.

The central conflict of *A Saintly Scent of Amber* is which Spanish convent will house the holy relics of her incorrupt body. History confirms the playwright's conceit: St. Teresa died and was buried in Alba de Tormes, later to be exhumed and brought to Ávila. Her incorrupt body remains there, while other relics have been returned to Alba, most notably the saint's pierced heart.

The scent of amber is gone, but St. Teresa's legend undoubtedly remains.

Kerri Allen
American Theatre Critics Association
Association Internacionale des Critiques de Théâtre

CAUTION: Professionals and amateurs are hereby warned that *A Saintly Scent of Amber*, being fully protected under the Copyright Laws of the United States of America, the British Empire, including the Dominion of Canada, and all other countries covered by the Pan-American Copyright Convention and the Universal Copyright Conventions, and of all countries with which the United States has reciprocal copyright relations, is subject to royalty. All rights, including professional, amateur, motion picture, recitation, public reading, radio and television broadcasting, and the rights of translation into foreign languages, are strictly reserved. Particular emphasis is laid on the question of readings, permission for which must be secured in writing. No part of this publication may be reproduced, stored in a retrieval system, or transmitted, in any form or by any means, without the prior permission in writing of ESTRENO Plays.

Inquiries regarding permissions should be addressed to the author through

D. Alfredo Carrión Saiz
Director de Artes Escénicas y Musicales
Sociedad General de Autores y Editores
Fernando VI, 4
28004 Madrid, SPAIN
Phone: 011-34-91-349-96-86   Fax: 011-34-91-349-97-12
E-mail: acarrion@sgae.es

or through the translator:

Karen Leahy
E-mail: kleahy@smith.alumnae.net
Phone: 646-262-1017

Un olor a ámbar (*A Saintly Scent of Amber*) was first staged in 1984 at the Ateneo in Madrid under the direction of Pablo Calvo. Principal roles were played by Tina Saíz, Manuel de Blas, Salvador Pons, Imma de Santis, Mercedes Lezcano and Tito Valverde. In 1984-85 the Calvo production was also staged at high school and university theatres in Madrid. Other stagings have followed in Madrid, Murcia, Zamora, and in 2002, under the direction of Miguel Nieto, in the Basílica de Santa Teresa in Alba de Tormes, the city near Salamanca where the historical events occurred. The first production outside Spain was performed in 1996 by Les Anachroniques at the University of Toulouse-Mirail in France, under the direction of Monique Martinez Thomas and Félix Martin Moral.

CHARACTERS:
(In order of appearance)

LAY SISTER 1
LAY SISTER 2
PRIORESS
INES
CATALINA
ISABEL
MARIA
JUANA
MARIANA
FATHER GRACIAN
BROTHER CRISTOBAL ALBERTO*
DOORKEEPER
GREGORIO
BROTHER ANTONIO

*Cristobal is pronounced like a combination of the following words: crease-TOW-bahl

[ ] Square brackets are used to indicate text from original publication omitted from the later acting version created by Les Anachroniques in Toulouse, France (1996).

ACT I

June 1583, Alba de Tormes, a provincial capital in Western Spain and site of the death of the Spanish mystic Saint Teresa of Avila (1515-1582). Convent of the Discalced Carmelites. Sacristy. A door, upstage left, Door A, leads to the chapel; a side door, stage right, Door B, leads to the interior rooms of the convent; another side door, stage left, Door C, leads to the entrance of the convent. There is a window upstage right.

Simple furnishings: a chest of drawers, a bench stage right and bench stage left, and a small table against the wall. Two lay sisters are cleaning the room; they are wearing long, dark skirts, thick black stockings, and large handkerchiefs on their heads.

LAY SISTER 1 (*Sweeping, she stops, leans on her broom, and sniffs the air*): Hey, do you smell that?

LAY SISTER 2: Shhh . . . (*With her index finger on her lips, she motions for LAY SISTER 1 to be quiet.*)

LAY SISTER 1: You don't have to answer out loud if you're doing penance. Just nod your head yes or no. Do you smell something?

(*LAY SISTER 2 gives a vigorous nod of her head, indicating "yes."*)

LAY SISTER 1: Oh, good! I thought I was just imagining it! In the short while I've been at this convent, that scent has yet to leave my nostrils.

(*While LAY SISTER 1 is still leaning on her broom, her gaze lost in the ceiling, the PRIORESS enters from Door A and crosses toward Door C.*)

PRIORESS: C'mon, c'mon! Get to work! No resting on your laurels! It's to be done today! What are you doing just standing there like a statue?

LAY SISTER 1: I was looking up at the ceiling, at that spider web. I was figuring out how to get rid of it.

PRIORESS: Well, with the broom on the ground and your eyes on the ceiling, all you can hope for is that it falls down. Watch this! (*She briskly takes the broom out of the hands of LAY SISTER 1 and picks up a rag from on top of the chest of drawers. She turns the broom upside down.*) You place the rag on top and you sweep the way you normally would, only upside down. (*The broom doesn't reach the ceiling.*) If you cannot reach the ceiling, stand on a chair. Here! (*She gives LAY SISTER 1 the broom back.*) No time to waste here. The masons are waiting for me. (*She exits.*)

LAY SISTER 2 (*Looking up at the ceiling*): I don't see a spider web.

LAY SISTER 1: How are you going to see one if there isn't one?

LAY SISTER 2: So, you lied?

LAY SISTER 1: Yeah, I lied, and you, you little tattletale, have broken your vow of silence. I had to make up something. I'm not that stupid nor have such bad manners that I would tell the Prioress the truth right to her face.

LAY SISTER 2: Oh, and what is the truth, if I may ask?

LAY SISTER 1: Well, what do you think it is? That I was standing here sniffing the air, because, in my opinion, this place has a strange, if not downright bad, smell.

LAY SISTER 2: So, how did you think up the story of the spider web?

LAY SISTER 1: Because of a story that my grandfather once told me. Since then, every time I look up at a ceiling, whether there's a spider web or not, I remember it.

LAY SISTER 2: Oh, do tell!

LAY SISTER 1: About my grandfather?

LAY SISTER 2: No, the story!

LAY SISTER 1: It's too long.

LAY SISTER 2: Tell me anyway. What was it about?

LAY SISTER 1: It was about a young woman who lived in Arcadia, who made such beautiful tapestries that she dared to challenge the very goddess of the arts—Minerva.

LAY SISTER 2: And the goddess accepted the challenge?

LAY SISTER 1: Yes.

LAY SISTER 2: And who won?

LAY SISTER 1: Hey, what's the deal here? Aren't you supposed to be doing penance?

LAY SISTER 2: Yes, but since I've already broken my vow, it no longer matters. Come on, tell me. Who won the challenge?

LAY SISTER 1: Who do you think won? The young girl, of course! If the goddess had won, it wouldn't be interesting, and the story wouldn't have been written, and my grandfather wouldn't have told it to me, and I wouldn't be telling it to you right now.

LAY SISTER 2: And the goddess? What did she do when she realized she had lost?

LAY SISTER 1: You are so annoying! Stop pestering me. If we keep this up, we'll get in trouble and there won't be any food for us at afternoon tea..

(*LAY SISTER 2 picks up the rag and begins to clean quickly.*)

LAY SISTER 2: All right. I'll clean, but you keep right on telling me the story, okay? Because if you don't finish, I won't be able to sleep tonight. And, just think how bad you'll feel.

LAY SISTER 1 (*Approaching LAY SISTER 2 and wagging her finger at her*): You just gotta know, don't you! (*She turns her back to LAY SISTER 2.*) I really don't like being pressured to tell a story, but I'll do it anyway, but only under one condition.

LAY SISTER 2: Whatever you want. (*She crosses to LAY SISTER 1.*)

LAY SISTER 1: That you give me half your food at afternoon tea.

LAY SISTER 2: Fine! We've got a deal. You can have the whole thing. Just tell the story. Please!

LAY SISTER 1: Okay, where was I?

LAY SISTER 2: The goddess Minerva had lost the competition. The young girl's tapestry was prettier than hers.

LAY SISTER 1: Ahh, yes! Then, Minerva got so angry that she decided to kill the young girl.

LAY SISTER 2: Are you kidding! How come? The poor thing!

LAY SISTER 1: Because of pride. What a paradox, don't you think? The young woman, a mere mortal, dares to challenge the art and knowledge of a goddess of Olympus, wins, and–

LAY SISTER 2: And she kills her?

LAY SISTER 1 (*Annoyed*): Nooo!

LAY SISTER 2: And that's how it ends? Then, what does the spider web have to do with the story?

LAY SISTER 1: If you keep on interrupting me, how can I get to it?

LAY SISTER 2: All right. I'll be quiet.

LAY SISTER 1: The young girl, who was very proud, wanted to die by her own hand. So, she took a rope, tied it to a beam, climbed up on a chair, and pushed the chair away.

LAY SISTER 2: How horrible! And what did Minerva do? Did she feel sorry for her and forgive her?

LAY SISTER 1: No! Don't be silly! [Just the opposite. When she saw the young woman was about to die, the cruel goddess didn't think simple death seemed like a severe enough punishment, so she decided to prolong her revenge. She touched the young girl with her magic wand and, while the poor girl was in the throes of death,] she made her smaller and smaller until she changed her into a spider, condemned to weave for century upon century the same pattern on the ceilings of all our homes.

LAY SISTER 2 (*Making the sign of the cross*): In the name of the Father, and of the Son, and of the Holy Ghost. Amen.

LAY SISTER 1: *What* are you doing?

LAY SISTER 2: It's a sin! A sin! We should not be talking about such things. They're pagan!

[**LAY SISTER 1**: Don't be so pious! It's only a story.

LAY SISTER 2: Tell me, what did the winning tapestry look like?

LAY SISTER 1: Hey, what happened to Miss Pious?

LAY SISTER 2: What do you expect? You've got me hooked! Since it's only a story, and since it was your grandfather who told it to you, it can't be that bad. Come on, details!

LAY SISTER 1: What? About my grandfather?

LAY SISTER 2: You're so mean! Not about your grandfather, the tapestry.

LAY SISTER 1: The tapestry? It was very beautiful, very beautiful. In the right-hand corner, the conquest of Europe by the bull.

LAY SISTER 2: I don't understand that. How is a bull going to conquer Europe?

LAY SISTER 1: Silly! Europe wasn't Spain, plus France, plus Italy. No. Europe was a beautiful woman. And the bull was Jupiter, the father of the gods. When she saw him in the meadow, so white, so handsome, so manly, with his horns and all, almost human, she walked right up to him, stroked his head, and when she saw that he was so tame, the silly girl climbed right up on his back. The bull, when he felt the touch of her skin on his back, began to run toward the sea. He crossed the ocean waters, while Europe, with her skirts lifted up by the wind and her head turned back toward the shore, called out desperately to her friends.

LAY SISTER 2: And was Jupiter married?

LAY SISTER 1: Yes, to the goddess, Juno, but he was always falling in love with other women. He did all kinds of crazy things when he fell in love, and jealousy made poor Juno carry out all sorts of cruel deeds.]

(*A bell rings, marking the recess hour, and immediately the voices of nuns are heard entering from the hallways on the right.*)

LAY SISTER 2: Hurry! They're coming! [Let's go! If they catch us here, we won't get any afternoon tea at all.

(*They pick up their things and go toward Door B.*)]

LAY SISTER 1 (*Pulling on LAY SISTER 2's arm*): No! Not through there!

(*They cross the stage and exit through Door C at the same time that a group of NUNS is entering, each one carrying [a low chair and] her sewing. The PRIORESS enters last.*)

PRIORESS: Settle yourselves as best you can. As long as the construction is going on, we have no choice but to use the sacristy as a sitting room. Open the window to let some light in, but do not make a lot of noise, the Provincial should be arriving at any moment.

(PRIORESS exits through Door C. Immediately, the nuns begin a happy chatter.)

INES OF JESUS: Will we all be able to make our confessions with him?

CATALINA: Well, if he does not have to leave immediately due to other concerns. Father Gracian is very kind. He will pluck time out of the air to make us happy.

ISABEL: I want to go first.

INES OF JESUS: None of that. We'll draw straws. In affairs of the soul, seniority shouldn't count.

ISABEL: Well now, the young ones are quite self-confident, don't you think?

MARIA OF SAINT FRANCIS: I've only confessed with him once, and he left my soul feeling like oil on troubled water.

CATALINA: I am also pleased that he is coming. And not only for confession, but also because, once and for all, we can clear up the issue of that mysterious scent. Without his permission, the Prioress can't take any action or make any decisions.

JUANA: Personally, I find it so distracting that when I am in the chapel, I can hardly even pray. Little by little it begins to seep into my pituitary gland, tingling me until I have to sneeze.

(JUANA sneezes. A chorus of God bless you's ensues.)

CATALINA: Oh Sister, do not say that without knowing for sure what it is. You could be saying something irreverent.

JUANA: I'm simply describing the effect that blessed scent has on my nose and soul. I don't think that saying the truth, here among ourselves, is irreverent.

CATALINA: I didn't mean to offend you, but imagine for a moment that the scent is not of this world, but rather is a message from heaven.

JUANA: Well, it's one of two things it seems: Either I am totally stupid and I don't get anything about anything, or a demon wants to enter my soul, and the sneeze, (*She sneezes.*) excuse me, scares him away.

MARIANA: As for me, and if I may be honest, it frightens me. Sometimes when I go into my cell at night, in the dark, and the scent is in there permeating everything, the sheets, the mattress, the walls, the pillow, I feel like crying and running out of there—I can't take it! (*She bursts into tears.*)

CATALINA: Don't cry. Don't be such a little girl. This nightmare will soon be over. If Mother Prioress does not speak with the Provincial, I promise you that we will do it ourselves.

(*INES stands and looks toward Door C.*)

INES OF JESUS: The Provincial! He's arrived! He's on his way here!

(*They all begin to whisper to one another. The PRIORESS enters, followed by FATHER GRACIAN and by BROTHER CRISTOBAL. Everyone stands up.*)

FATHER GRACIAN: How are you, my children?

EVERYONE (*In a chorus*): Very well, Father, thank you. And Your Reverence, how are you? Have you had a good trip?

FATHER GRACIAN: I cannot complain about my health. I am in better health than I deserve and than I would have ever dreamed. And, the trip was splendid. And although it is the beginning of June, the weather has been like spring, neither hot nor cold. Isn't that so, Brother Cristobal Alberto?

BROTHER CRISTOBAL: Yes, it is, Father Gracian.

FATHER GRACIAN: But please sit down, all of you. Do not remain standing.

(*The NUNS sit down and, at a gesture from the PRIORESS, the BROTHERS also sit down, on a bench, stage left.*)

PRIORESS (*Still standing to the right*): As you all know, Father Gracian was a personal friend of Mother Teresa of Jesus. He was her confessor and he accompanied her on all her trips as she established the new convents. Father Gracian felt deep sorrow that he was not present at the hour of her death, and he wishes to hear the details regarding her last days at this convent and what she said before she died. Therefore, I implore those of you who were with her to be charitable enough to share this with him. Speak simply and truthfully, and try to console him as best you can. In fact, the Reverend has been so eager to speak with all of you that he has not wanted to eat or drink. So, Catalina, please go to the kitchen and bring out something to eat.

FATHER GRACIAN: Don't bother, Sister.

CATALINA (*From Door B*): It is no bother, Father. I am pleased to be able to serve you. You both must be famished after such a long trip.

PRIORESS: Let it not be said that the Convent of Alba does not treat its very own Provincial royally.

FATHER GRACIAN: Do as you like, Mother. I do not wish to rule in the kitchen.

(*The group falls silent.*)

PRIORESS: Very well, does anyone wish to begin? (*The NUNS give little smiles and murmurs of embarrassment.*) Mariana of the Incarnation!

(*MARIANA stands up.*) Father, Mariana is the daughter of Antonio Gaytan.

FATHER GRACIAN: Come here, my child, so that I may have a good look at you. (*MARIANA takes a hesitant step towards him.*) Yes, you give the same look and have the same smile. An extraordinary man—your father! You can be proud of him. Even though he was a married man, with a wife and children, he left his family for extended periods of time in order to accompany Mother Teresa down God's sacred paths. I met him during the founding of the convent of Beas, and then we were together during the founding of the convent in Seville. Ah, Seville! [Oh, how they made us suffer, those people. There were so many obstacles and so much slander and gossip. And it was all so exaggerated and yet so well put together that I don't know how we managed to get out of there free from the hands of the Inquisition. But let's not dwell on such unpleasant and distant memories.] Tell me, my child, did you speak with her?

MARIANA: Yes, Father, I accompanied her to her bed. She could barely stand up, and she said to me, "It has been so long since I have gone to bed so early!" And she fell, the poor thing, flat on the ground. Even with two of us, we were not able to budge her to turn her over. I was so traumatized that the Prioress permitted me not to return to her cell. I am such a coward, Father!

FATHER GRACIAN: It is not cowardice, my child, it is youth, and at your age death seems so strange and far away. You have not yet comprehended the dimension of time, the lightening flash in which time passes; but when you are twice your age, and you look back, you will say, "All of these years have not lasted more than a sigh." And from all of them, only a little mound of feelings and memories will remain, along with the satisfaction of having fulfilled your obligations. Sit down, my child!

(*CATALINA enters with two partridges and a pitcher of wine; INES grabs the tray and takes it to FATHER GRACIAN and BROTHER CRISTOBAL.*)

FATHER GRACIAN (*continued*): It is not a simple meal. But, on this occasion, I will say just as Mother Teresa once said to a peasant man, "Do not be scandalized, my brother, penitence is one thing and partridges quite another."

PRIORESS: Catalina! (*CATALINA gets up.*)

CATALINA: Within only a few days of being on her sick bed, Mother Teresa asked, quite insistently, for the Blessed Sacrament.

PRIORESS (*Stammering*): I . . . at first . . . denied her, fearing that she would throw it up. She was in such a state! I told her that she should wait until the next morning, but she would not allow it. Fortunately, her stomach handled it well.

CATALINA: When the Body of Christ came through the door, she sat up, without the help of anyone, with such force that it appeared as if she were going to leap out of bed. The color returned to her face and it seemed to take on a healthy glow. And she repeated over and over, "Oh, Lord, my Husband. The hour that I have awaited for so long has arrived. It is now time for us to be together." And she gave many thanks to God because she was dying within the Church. She also said that we should not imitate her example, that she had been a bad nun. (*She sits down.*)

ISABEL (*Getting up*): She spoke to us very tenderly and emphasized the keeping of her Rules and Constitutions. And she recited verses from it: "Ne projicias me a facie tua." Then she was silent for a long time until she entered into agony.

JUANA (*Getting up*): When her death drew near, we heard a crowd of people in the cloister, and we understood that they were saints from the Order (to which she was very devoted) and that they had come to carry her soul away. (*She sits down.*)

MARIA (*Getting up*): She died between nine and ten at night, the day of Saint Francis. As soon as she expired, her skin smoothed out and she seemed younger than she was. She had the appearance of a venerable man rather than that of a woman, perhaps because of the serenity of her face or because of a light covering of hair that appeared on her chin.

INES (*Poetic*): Her feet were transformed into mother-of-pearl. They were almost transparent. An intense aroma inundated the cell and we had to open the window because we could not tolerate it. It was so strong that even Sister Catalina Baptist, who had lost her sense of smell months before, was able to smell it. And it was not only in the cell, but also in the entire house and especially on the objects that Mother had touched—on the salt shaker and on her toothpicks.

FATHER GRACIAN: What did it smell like?

INES: I don't know, Father. It was not always exactly the same. It's just like the scent that is coming out of her crypt right now. (*She claps her hand over her mouth, as if she has revealed a big secret.*)

FATHER GRACIAN (*To the PRIORESS*): What does she mean by that?

PRIORESS (*Stammering*): I was planning to speak to you. . . precisely. . . about that, Reverend. But Sister Ines mentioned it before I had the opportunity. It is a matter that has upset the convent a great deal. The scent is always in the chapel. And on Sundays and feast days, it permeates the entire house, and there is not one place, not even the kitchen or the washroom, where you cannot smell it. It lingers on the flowers, the benches, the curtains, and even on freshly scrubbed floors.

FATHER GRACIAN: Are you certain that it is emanating from the crypt?

PRIORESS: Without a doubt. The closer you get the more intense the smell.

FATHER GRACIAN: Perhaps she wasn't buried correctly.

PRIORESS: That's simply not possible. I personally called on Pedro Barajas, who is in charge of the burials for the House of Alba. I made certain that he buried the casket deep in the earth, and that he covered it with an abundance of soil, as much as if he were digging the foundation for a house. We were afraid that someone would try to disinter her.

FATHER GRACIAN: And her body was not treated before it was placed in the casket?

PRIORESS: No. It was buried without removing any of the organs. There was no embalming, nor was there any other artifice applied to her body. We placed her in the coffin dressed only in her habit, and seven hours after her death she was interred. We buried her so quickly that her brother-in-law and sister were upset because they did not arrive in time to view her body.

FATHER GRACIAN: And why were you in such a hurry to bury her?

PRIORESS: I already told you, Father. We were afraid that someone would disinter the casket and want to take her body. This city and this convent would deeply regret that, since we consider her body to be that of a saint.

BROTHER CRISTOBAL: Might this not be a message from Mother Teresa? She was fond of pleasant scents, and appreciated the fact that she was given perfumes to sprinkle on the Lord's altar.

FATHER GRACIAN: Yes, it's possible. I do remember on one occasion that a woman approached her on the street to kiss her hands, and she said, "Oh, Lord, what a lovely smell comes from the hands of this saint!"

PRIORESS: I humbly suggest that we exhume her body, and that we discover once and for all the cause of this mysterious odor. Our sisters would regain their tranquility, and community life would regain its regular rhythm, without this state of unease and frazzled nerves.

FATHER GRACIAN: Nothing would please me more than to see and to touch the remains of Mother Teresa. And since I could not attend to her in her last hours, at the very least, I would be pleased to collaborate with you, allowing her body to rest in peace by eliminating any doubts. Did you notice anything unusual after her death?

CATALINA: She appeared to me with a ribbon in hand, and with that ribbon she was bound to God.

PRIORESS: Another time, the day of The Holy Innocents, when the sisters were in morning prayers, she appeared to them. They saw that a crown, like a tiara, had been placed on her head, and that her face was lit up like an angel and filled with humility.

FATHER GRACIAN: Well then I believe that we have sufficient cause. Where is the tomb?

PRIORESS: In the chapel, in a space in the lower choir stalls. It's on the other side of this wall. (*She points to a spot next to Door A.*) This is the back wall. Smell, smell, Reverend, and it's not even Sunday.

(*FATHER GRACIAN approaches and smells.*)

FATHER GRACIAN: Yes, there is certainly a smell, although I cannot identify the smell, nor if it is pleasant or unpleasant. Smell, smell, Brother Cristobal.

BROTHER CRISTOBAL (*Sniffing close to the wall*): It smells like musk or rosemary.

FATHER GRACIAN: Reverend Mother, let's exhume the body.

PRIORESS (*Happily*): There are masons in the convent, making some repairs. I will call them.

FATHER GRACIAN: No, Reverend Mother, do not call them. This shouldn't be made public until we get to the heart of the matter.

PRIORESS: As you wish. Mariana, Ines, go and get picks and shovels; Isabel, baskets for the dirt and brooms to sweep with. Juana, spread a sheet on the floor. Catalina, you take charge of her habit and the casket. (*Addressing the BROTHERS.*) Come this way.

(*The PRIORESS, followed by the BROTHERS, exits through Door A. Enter MARIANA and INES.*)

MARIANA: Here are the pickaxes.

INES: And the shovels.

(*INES turns to leave by Door A. MARIANA stops. She is frightened.*)

MARIANA (*Handing her the pickaxes*): Take them, please. I'm scared.

(*Exit INES. MARIANA slips into a corner. Sounds of picks and shovels during this entire scene. Enter JUANA with the sheet. Enter INES through Door A.*)

JUANA: Where should I put it?

INES: On the floor. It's for the bones.

(*MARIANA grimaces in horror. Enter the two LAY SISTERS with the casket. They place it on the sheet.*)

ISABEL (*Entering with the basket and the broom*): Wait, what are you doing? Not on the sheet! No! Take it off! Put it somewhere else!

LAY SISTER 1 (*To LAY SISTER 2*): Didn't I tell you that the smell was strange? There's going to be trouble. I know what I'm talking about.

(*Exit the two LAY SISTERS.*)

PRIORESS (*From the door, with her sleeves rolled up and with a shovel in her hand*): Hurry up. The basket. We're getting covered with dirt. (*ISABEL runs toward the PRIORESS.*) And the rest of you, don't just stand there. Do something. Pray at least.

(*INES and MARIANA fall to their knees and begin to pray. Enter JUANA and she joins them. Enter CATALINA shortly after with a habit in her hands. She places it on the chest of drawers and she kneels also.*)

PRIORESS (*Shouting*): Stop! Stop! Father, you're already there! Careful with the pickaxe! You may damage it! Relax for the love of God!

(*FATHER GRACIAN and BROTHER CRISTOBAL appear through Door A, being pushed by the PRIORESS back into the sacristy. They are sweaty and have the sleeves of their habits rolled up.*) Ines accompany the Brothers. Let them clean up a little. (*Exit the three through Door B.*) Come, sisters. We'll get her out ourselves. The rest of you, come here.

(*The remaining NUNS enter, curious, all except for MARIANA who hangs back half–hidden on the side of the chest of drawers with her hands covering her ears so she can't hear the conversation which comes through to the sacristy very clearly from inside the chapel.*)

PRIORESS: Use your hands . . . just your hands, to take off the dirt! Like this, to the right! To the right! Not so hard! Easy! Easy . . . It's out. Clean it off a little on top. Good! Good! All right, now we'll take it into the sacristy. Hold on tight. Ready, one, two, three!

(*The PRIORESS, CATALINA, ISABEL, and JUANA enter through Door A with the coffin on their shoulders. MARIA walks behind them.*)

PRIORESS: All right, here on the sheet so we don't stain the floor. Slowly, carefully . . . good. (*They place it on the sheet.*) Maria, bring another sheet.

(*MARIA takes a sheet out of the chest of drawers and opens it over to one side. CATALINA leans over the coffin.*)

CATALINA: One of the boards is broken (*She lifts it off.*) and dirt has gotten inside.

ISABEL: The wood is moldy and half-rotten.

PRIORESS (*To MARIA who is nosing around*): Give me the basket for the boards. (*INES enters.*) Let's take off the lid. (*CATALINA and ISABEL help her.*)

ISABEL: You can't see anything. It's all covered in dirt.

(*They put the lid on the floor. The PRIORESS looks over at MARIANA affectionately and walks over to her. The PRIORESS takes her by the shoulders and guides MARIANA to the foot of the coffin.*)

PRIORESS: Mariana, my child, why don't you go to her first and reconcile yourself with death. We are what we'll be: bones, skull, and skeleton dressed in strips of skin that cover our souls while we are exiled to this temporal world. And in the end, we are nothing, just a little mold and a handful of dirt. It is much easier to renounce all that is worldly while staring at a skull.

(*MARIANA, with her eyes closed and while trembling, leans forward and then with great effort reopens her eyes.*)

MARIANA: I don't see anything, Mother, only her habit and some dirt. (*Forcing herself, she slowly lifts the habit. She drops it quickly and covers her mouth to hold back a scream. The PRIORESS, who is right behind her, leans towards her afraid that she is going to faint.*) Feet! Feet! Her feet! (*She moves away terrorized. She backs away and then moves back forward and runs out through Door C. She continues screaming.*) Her feet! Her feet!

(*FATHER GRACIAN and BROTHER CRISTOBAL enter through Door B.*)

PRIORESS: And her legs! And her abdomen! And her breast!

FATHER GRACIAN (*Nervously touching his habit*): And her arms? Where are her arms?

CATALINA: Here is the left one. It's whole! Absolutely whole!

FATHER GRACIAN: And here is the right one. The hand is hidden by dirt and limestone, but it is whole too.

BROTHER CRISTOBAL: The fingers! Pinky! Ring! Middle! Index! And thumb!

INES and ISABEL (*Jumping up and down*): Miracle! Miracle! Miracle! Miraaaaaaacle!

CATALINA: I cannot take off her veil. It is stuck to her face like a second skin.

PRIORESS: Do not pull, Sister. You don't want to skin her. Let's get water, water and towels; let's wash her.

(*ISABEL exits running.*)

FATHER GRACIAN (*He touches her and gets up*): She is incorrupt. No question.

BROTHER CRISTOBAL: This incorruption can't be natural either, principally because she's a woman and in her case somewhat stout. Women are very moist and luscious with humidity—very suitable to "ad corruptionem."

FATHER GRACIAN: Let us give thanks to the Lord for having preserved her body. Whether it is a miracle or a whim of nature, the consequences are the same for the future of the Reforms and for the prestige of our Mother, so spoken about throughout her lifetime and which will now continue to be after her death. The exact same doctrine from someone who isn't a saint versus someone who is, just does not have the same impact. Nor should we forget that our Mother's writings are still in the hands of the Inquisition. Perhaps this is the message of her body, to demonstrate to the world at large the orthodoxy and veracity of Mother Teresa of Jesus, founder of the Discalced Carmelites. (*He crosses himself.*) Hail Mary, full of grace, the Lord is with thee. Blessed art thou amongst women and blessed is the fruit of thy womb, Jesus.

CHORUS OF NUNS: Holy Mary, mother of God, pray for us sinners, now and at the hour of our death. Amen. Jesus.

(*ISABEL enters with a jug of water in one hand and a washbasin and towel in the other.*)

PRIORESS: Excuse me, Your Reverences, may I please entreat you both to go out for just a moment. We need to disrobe her to change her habit.

FATHER GRACIAN: Why, of course. (*They exit through Door B.*)

PRIORESS: Help me lift her up. Be careful! Extremely careful! Do not accidentally break her arms.

CATALINA: My goodness, how her hair has grown. It is even coming out through the veil of her habit.

ISABEL: She doesn't weigh a thing. She's like a doll.

CATALINA: It is the weight of blessed flesh.

PRIORESS: Perhaps it would be more respectable to disrobe her in the chapel. Let's take her there.

(*The PRIORESS and ISABEL take her through Door A. CATALINA takes the habit from on top of the chest of drawers and INES takes the jug of water and the washbasin. The conversation from within the chapel can be clearly heard.*)

ISABEL: Look, sisters, I can keep her standing with just one finger to hold her up.

PRIORESS: Careful, careful, she might fall.

MARIA: I can't get the veil off her face. Even with some water, it does not come off.

ISABEL: Let's try with a little wine. It's stronger. (*She comes back on stage, takes the wine off the tray, and re-exits through Door A.*)

CATALINA: Her skin is covered in a fine oil.

INES: It's coming off now. I can see her forehead, chin, and mouth.

ISABEL: Her nose! What happened to her nose? It looks sunken.

PRIORESS: Not sunken, broken. It's because of a board. The lid broke it. It got her right on the face.

INES: Oh, what a shame, considering how well preserved the whole rest of her body is.

PRIORESS: Her face, hands, and feet are darkened as if they had been burned by the limestone, but take a look at her belly, see what an immaculate white it is.

INES: If I'm close to her, she smells like amber or ambrosia, and if I move away (*As she moves away her back is seen through the door into the sacristy.*), the fragrance is supremely delicate, like fresh roses.

ISABEL (*Entering with the habit to place it in the basket*): The habit smells bad, but the slip (*She tosses it onto the sheet.*) that was flush up against her has the same aroma as her body.

PRIORESS (*Entering with the body in her arms*): Isabel, go and burn the habit and put away the rest. If this turns out to be a miracle, they will be relics.

ISABEL (*Calling out as she exits through Door B*): Father, Father, you may both come in now.

PRIORESS: Look, she can practically stand up with just one finger holding her.

(*FATHER GRACIAN and BROTHER CRISTOBAL enter. They look at Mother Teresa and touch her.*)

FATHER GRACIAN: Her skin gives as if she were alive. She was pretty stout. See, look at her girth.

PRIORESS: Well, she tasted neither wine nor meat. She would nourish herself with a bowl of lentils and one egg. And, at times sardines. On occasion, I would hear her say that, if they'd let her, she would nourish herself with only acorns like they do with the pigs.

(*ISABEL enters running.*)

ISABEL: Miracle! Miracle! Miracle . . . miracle!

PRIORESS: Calm down, my child, calm down. What's happened?

ISABEL (*Nervous and breathless*): As you ordered me to, I threw the boards and the habit into the chimney. When they began to burn, they let off a smell so disagreeable that I couldn't take it. Suddenly, the flames separated from the boards and floated through the room like clouds. I thought I was going to be scorched to death, but my feet were so planted on the ground, I wasn't able to flee. I knelt down on my knees imploring our Mother Teresa for help, and then the flames like children who have heard the voice of their mother, obediently returned, one by one, into the chimney.

FATHER GRACIAN: Store that in your memory, my child. It could be useful in the future. (*He lifts Mother Teresa's veil and takes a peek.*) She is in perfect condition, except for her nose.

CATALINA: Mother, I have wrapped her slip in a sheet and the sheet is now seeped in the same oil. I have changed the sheet three or four times and they, too, have become drenched. It is as if this substance never runs out.

PRIORESS: Don't wash those sheets. Store them with the slip. Father, could we put her back in the casket?

FATHER GRACIAN: Yes, I'll help you. (*They place her inside. The PRIORESS takes the lid with the intention of closing the casket.*) No, not yet. I would like a few moments alone with her.

PRIORESS: My children, please come with me.

(*All the NUNS exit.*)

FATHER GRACIAN: You too, please, Brother Cristobal. (*BROTHER CRISTOBAL stays spying; every once in awhile his head peeks out to look.*) I haven't stayed just to talk to you. You're probably up to snuff with what they're plotting to do with the Reforms anyway. They want to modify the Constitution, in twenty places, no less. You put me in charge of not letting them change even a single comma. And, while I am still able, I will continue to try. But, among the insiders, we have the absolute worst enemies. There is whispering about me and Maria of San Jose, just like there was about you and me by those "calced ravens," as you called them. And, I don't know how to defend myself, which makes things all the worse. I'm afraid they are going to be able to out maneuver me. Juan of the Cross has told me that not only will they take away my position, but if they could they would also take away my habit. I fear nothing for myself and am perfectly willing to suffer for the cause, if it is God's will. Well, anyway, to change the subject, and I'll tell you without beating around the bush, I've stayed here only to take with me your hand so that it may accompany me in my sufferings, which most certainly await me. (*Joking.*) Will you give me your permission, Dorotea? Now don't get angry, since you were the one who gave yourself that nickname, and I don't imagine that you would have lost your sense of humor in heaven. (*He takes out a knife, and cuts off a hand and then looking one way and then the other like a thief, he wraps it in a handkerchief and puts it in a pocket. He then pulls down the sleeve of the habit so that it is not noticeable and after putting the lid back on the casket, exits speaking.*) Pray up there for me, dear Dorotea! (*He exits through Door C.*)

(*BROTHER CRISTOBAL who sees him leave, enters. Furtively, looking both ways, he takes off the lid of the casket again, holding a knife in his hand.*)

BROTHER CRISTOBAL: If the Provincial took a hand, I, as his assistant, would have the right to take something. I'll cut off a little finger or just a toe from her foot, perhaps her pinky toe, so that I will not be committing the sin of ambition.

(*He lifts up her habit, cuts a little toe off her foot and puts it in a pocket without wrapping it; meanwhile the bells begin to ring loudly and joyously. Frightened, he runs out through Door C after quickly shutting the casket.*)

(*The stage remains empty for a moment, with only the sound of the ringing bells. The PRIORESS enters through Door B and walks in the direction of Door C. She stops for a moment center stage.*)

PRIORESS: Ring the bells louder so the whole town of Alba recognizes that a saint is born!

ACT II

The PRIORESS'S office. A door halfway upstage left (C). A door halfway upstage right leads to the interior of the convent (B). A sideways table at an angle stage left. The table has been pulled off its platform and the platform is stage right in the back corner on a diagonal. A pair of easy chairs and some straight-backed chairs. A window in the back. A small bookcase.

This platform, on which the table/desk is normally situated, has been used to create a little theatre stage with curtains made out of dark cloth with a pattern of white lilies painted on it. Hanging from up above it, in the center, is a white dove. LAY SISTER 1 opens and closes the curtains to assess the effect.

LAY SISTER 1: Perfect! It's come out, absolutely perfect! The yellow's run a little, but from far away you don't notice a thing.

LAY SISTER 2 (*She enters holding a Classical Roman costume in her arms; she places it behind the curtains*): They're going to make Mother Teresa a saint! San Juan's prior, Fernando of Toledo, has put forth a mountain of ducats so as to begin the process.

LAY SISTER 1: The documents from Rome cost a lot of money and Rome is also really far away!

LAY SISTER 2: If, one day, it makes it to the altar, Alba will become the capital of Spain. What am I talking about, not just Spain! There'll be pilgrimages from all over the world and even the Pope himself will leave the Vatican to admire her.

LAY SISTER 1: The church moves slowly. It can be years, even centuries .

ISABEL (*Entering*): None of that century stuff. The issue is moving along quite swiftly. The Duchess of Alba has already charged someone with the making of the coffin to display her body. It's very rich and luxurious—lined with crimson damask on the inside and on the outside it's velvet, adorned with very expensive gold-plated nails. [It has a little matching velvet pillow with a taffeta ruffle embroidered in gold. Oh yeah, and a little throw to place over our Mother.]

INES (*Entering*): And Father Francisco de Rivera of the Society of Jesus, who was her confessor, is writing a book about all of her miracles. The ones that happened while she was alive and the ones that are now happening with her body.

CATALINA (*Entering*): News flash! News flash! The Bishop of Salamanca has begun to do private interviews with all the people who knew her. Soon he'll come to this convent.

ISABEL (*Runs to the table and raps on it*): Attention, attention! Silence! This is a dress rehearsal! Imagine that I am the Bishop of Salamanca who has come to interview each one of you. (*Putting on a fake voice.*) Sister Catalina of Jesus. Come forward. Do you swear to tell the truth, the whole truth, and nothing but the truth, so help you God?

CATALINA: I do.

ISABEL: Did you meet Mother Teresa of Jesus?

CATALINA: Yes, My Most Reverend. Two or three times when she was visiting in Alba.

ISABEL: And did the Lord, our Father, enact any miracles through her being?

CATALINA: Yes, sir. I know of them. Many. There have been many. Let's see... where to begin? (*She scratches her head trying to recall.*) There are so many. Oh, now I remember. During the onset of the founding of the Discalced Carmelites, the nuns wore sackcloth tunics made of very coarse wool-like horse blankets. So, since they were natural, lots of lice bred in them. The nuns could not eat, sleep, or even gather together in prayer. The influx of these little guests was so great and they reproduced with such swiftness that the poor nuns were desperate. And since they did not have enough hands to alleviate the itch, they turned to Mother Teresa in search of help.

ISABEL: Interesting! Interesting! And, what did Mother Teresa do?

CATALINA: Our Mother was a gifted writer. She was very funny. She made up a prayer and the nuns went around the convent for two days chanting it.

ISABEL: Do you remember the lyrics?

CATALINA: How did it begin? Well, give us all a new dress . . .

(*All the NUNS chant in chorus except for ISABEL.*)

CATALINA and CHORUS OF NUNS:
Well, give us all a new dress,
Oh, most celestial of kings.
Free us from this bad mess,
And give us new, clean things.

CATALINA (*Chanting*):
Quiet these evil little vermin
Whose spirits do not put a lot of emotion
Into your loyal and faithful devotion.

CATALINA and CHORUS:
Free us from this bad mess,
And give us new, clean things.

CATALINA *(Chanting)*:
You came to this Earth to die,
So do not be fearful,
And do not faint,
Each one of these nuns is a saint.

CATALINA and CHORUS OF NUNS:
Well, give us all a new dress,

Oh, most celestial of kings.
Free us from this bad mess,
And give us new, clean things.

CATALINA: From then on, the lice disappeared, which was, and still is, considered a real miracle, since those minute, resistant, and infectious bloody little buggers are so hard to get rid of.

ISABEL: Thank you, Sister Catalina. You may be seated. Sister Ines of Jesus. (*INES approaches.*) Do you swear to tell the truth, the whole truth, and nothing but the truth?

INES: I swear.

ISABEL: Do you know the question?

INES: Yes, Your Most Reverend.

ISABEL: Well, just begin then, this way we can keep it brief.

INES: [Your Most Reverend, I am going to recount to you a miracle that really had a big impact on me.] When they exhumed our Mother, Father Gracian[, who was the provincial at the time,] cut off one of her hands and took it with him to Lisbon. There, in that very city, lived a gentleman who was jealous and did not trust his wife. He was so tormented by this passion that one evil day, he decided to kill her. [He waited for the dark of night. Being neither short-sighted nor indolent, he premeditated with absolute treachery and stealthily placed a knife under his pillow. And] once she was sleeping he put the knife just above her heart ready to tear out her soul when he remembered Mother Teresa of Jesus and ran to the convent asking for help [even though it was the early hours of dawn and was stormy outside.] The Prioress [who was Mother Maria of San Jose] lent him the hand so that he could put it under his pillow. And, oh what a miracle, first a great tranquility overcame him and then a restorative slumber. He fell asleep immediately and the next morning, completely transformed, he threw away the knife and reconciled with his wife. Together they made a novena as a prayer of petition and from then on they ate partridges and lived happily ever after.

SABEL: You should really get rid of the "happily ever after" and the "eating partridges." They don't really go with such a passionate tale. It loses, how might one say this . . . it loses its . . . authenticity. That's it—authenticity. Please be seated, Sister. Let's see. You two, approach, please. (*To the LAY SISTERS.*) Who has been at the convent longer?

LAY SISTER 1: Your humble servant.

SABEL: Have you seen or heard of any miracles that have occurred from Mother Teresa's relics?

LAY SISTER 1: Yes, Your Most Reverend. Not more than two months ago, a nobleman from town, named Francisco of Cardenas, had so hurt his head that they could pull out rotten shards from it. He'd been out of it for two years. Would you believe it? He would go around saying he was the Cid. His poor family didn't even realize what was happening! When the Prioress found out, she sent a little cloth tinged with the oil from Mother Teresa's body to his wife. And, when they cured him with the oil, they managed to pull a rotten piece out of his head this big. They placed the cloth on his wound and he began to get better and better. And now, he responds to his Christian name and doesn't even remember anything about the Cid.

SABEL (*Addressing LAY SISTER 2*): Did you know Mother Teresa?

LAY SISTER 2: No, sir, I never had the pleasure, but I saw her after she was dead. She has been well preserved. Fabulously well preserved. But, look here, Your Most Reverend, let me be honest with you. I can't really put together a whole story in full detail. However, in the time I've been here[, I have heard that] she has cured pox, burning fevers, fatigue, hot flashes, stomachaches, leg aches and backaches, abscesses in the throat, leg pain, foot pain, heart pain, eye pain, side pain, jaw pain, fainting, trembling, blindness, cramps, and I don't even know what else, which I can't really come up with right at this moment.

(*MARIANA enters running.*)

MARIANA: She's coming! She's coming! She's here, she's here!

(They all run and hide behind the theatre stage's curtains.)

NUNS (*In unison*): Happy birthday, Mother Prioress!

PRIORESS: So that's what it was! I said to myself this morning that something strange was going on.

ISABEL: [We hope you are not displeased.] We wanted to surprise you and there was no better place than in here. [We've made special use of the platform.]

PRIORESS: No, my child, I am not displeased. On the contrary, I don't deserve all this.

(The little bell from the doorkeeper's office rings. The DOORKEEPER goes out to answer the door.)

CATALINA (*Addressing the two LAY SISTERS, INES, and ISABEL*): Come on, get going. Go inside and prepare.

PRIORESS: Such pretty curtains! Who painted them?

MARIANA: Sister Isabel.

PRIORESS: I had no idea she had such talent. How did you get the paints?

MARIANA: I think she made them out of limestone, egg yolk, and oil.

PRIORESS: Ingenious. I see you have all prepared a full out performance. What is the play about?

MARIANA: It's a secret. All I can say is that it is the debut of this play here at this convent and we've spent more than two weeks in preparation. And, don't think it has been easy to find the time and dodge your watchful eye.

PRIORESS: Mea culpa, mea culpa! How poorly I do my duty if you managed to pull all this off without me finding out.

MARIANA: The night is long and we took hours off our sleep. Don't think that we took time away from our prayers or our duties.

(*The DOORKEEPER enters and directs herself to the PRIORESS.*)

DOORKEEEPER: Reverend Mother, a man has come saying his name is Pedro Vallejo and that he is a judge for the Duke of Alba. His little son, who is just three years old, is suffering. He won't eat, cry, laugh, or talk. The poor man is desperate and has tearfully requested a relic of Mother Teresa.

PRIORESS: Give him one. Take a piece of her slip from the trunk.

CATALINA (*Poking through her pockets*): Don't bother, Sister. Here is a little piece of her skin that came off while washing her back.

(*She gives it to her. The DOORKEEPER exits running.*)

PRIORESS: Let us pray so that God will take pity on him. Our Father, who art in Heaven, hallowed be Thy name. Thy kingdom come, Thy will be done, on Earth as it is in Heaven.

CHORUS OF NUNS: Give us this day our daily bread. And forgive us our trespasses, as we forgive those who trespass against us. And lead us not into temptation, but deliver us from evil. Amen.

(*The DOORKEEPER enters.*)

DOORKEEPER: He departed quite relieved.

PRIORESS: We trust that he shall be saved.

CATALINA: Mother, may we begin?

PRIORESS: Whenever you'd like.

(They bring the PRIORESS a chair. The rest sit on the floor. Silence. The curtain opens. It is a jail cell. INES is crouching in one corner, dressed in white with a luxurious shawl. She stands up and crosses to center stage.)

INES: My name is Coloma, which means dove in Latin. I was born in Spain at the end of the third century, in a city near the Pyrenees Mountains. My parents were noble and rich—see, look at my shawl— but they were pagan. One day my childhood friends and I planned to sneak out of the house and cross the border into France. I had heard that Emperor Aurelius's sojourn there had intensified the persecution of the Christians. So we did it. My companions had more luck than I did, and were martyred quickly. Being a woman, however, I have thus far been spared my life in order that I be forced into renouncing my faith. They have kept me here, behind bars, for many long days, praying and waiting impatiently for the sword that will behead me.

(LAY SISTER 1 enters dressed like a Roman and takes a tough stance.)

LAY SISTER 1: The Emperor Aurelius!

(INES shrinks fearfully. ISABEL enters dressed as an emperor and she motions to the soldier to withdraw. The SOLDIER leaves bowing. AURELIUS looks at COLOMA carefully, circling around her. He grabs her hair and twists her head brusquely so he can see her profile.)

ISABEL (Aurelius): Beautiful bone structure, yes sir. Appropriately Roman. A gorgeous profile, strong and sure without any hesitancy. Eyes of almond and honey, hair of golden lemon. How they will shine in the temple I've erected to the sun god! What are you called?

INES (Coloma): Coloma.

ISABEL (Aurelius): Columba, you mean. Well, it's the same thing in that local jargon you speak around here. Your friends are dead, you know?

INES (Coloma): Yes.

ISABEL (Aurelius): You know you are right behind them if you persist in adoring that pathetic parched and starving man who died on the cross.

INES (Coloma): I know that.

ISABEL (Aurelius): Do you not like the Roman gods, little girl? Are you not roused by Minerva, goddess of wisdom and the arts? And what about the hunter, Diana? Or the beautiful Venus? Or Jupiter? Ah, if only Jupiter could see you! And, what about Neptune, the god of the sea? Or Vesta or Mercury? And, Apollo? He is very handsome, you know. Or is it that you do not like men, either? Well, then you would surely like Ceres, the great mother. As you can see, you can choose without any worries. There are many different choices for all tastes and preferences.

INES (Coloma): I neither can nor want to choose, because my God, the one and only true God, has chosen me.

ISABEL (Aurelius): Do you not fear death? Do you not fear beasts and fire?

INES (Coloma): I fear nothing because the love of Christ fills me with strength.

ISABEL (Aurelius): I am warning you, little girl, that love will be your ruin.

INES (Coloma): I worship and accept Jesus Christ as my savior.

ISABEL (Aurelius): Well, no one is preventing you from that. You can worship in silence and pretend that you believe in the gods of the Empire. Your life is well worth a lie. In Rome, we have always been very tolerant, very liberal, with all our beliefs. Many of our gods, what am I saying, actually the majority of our gods, are imported from elsewhere. But, your situation is different. This Jesus endeavors to destroy the foundation of the Roman State. That is why he has been proclaimed as public enemy number one. Rome has decreed a battle to the death against all his supporters. So, wise up, little girl. You either renounce your faith now or I will have you dishonored.

INES (Coloma): Almighty God, whom I love and adore, will grant that I die a virgin.

ISABEL (Aurelius): Ha, ha, ha, ha. We'll see about that. Soldier! Sooooldier!

(*LAY SISTER 1 appears immediately with a tough demeanor.*)

LAY SISTER 1 (Soldier): At your orders, my Emperor.

ISABEL (Aurelius): Take this maiden's virginity away. Do not hesitate. And, then fill me in on what has occurred. (*To COLOMA.*) You are too stubborn, worse than stubborn. I would have preferred not to harm you, but one does not contradict the Emperor of Rome, and even less so, a little brat like you. (*To SOLDIER.*) She says that her God will impede you from doing it. (*Exits.*)

(*The SOLDIER places his spearhead calmly in a corner and takes off his helmet and leaves it on the floor. He approaches INES. She kneels and prays.*)

INES (Coloma): Mary most pure, conceived without sin, pray for me. Hail Mary, full of grace, the Lord is with thee, blessed are thou amongst women and blessed is the fruit of thy womb, Jesus. Holy Mary . . .

LAY SISTER 1 (Soldier): If you do not resist, little one, all will go well. Lie down on your back.

INES (Coloma): Oh my dear God, come to my aid. Do not permit me to transgress against You.

LAY SISTER 1 (Soldier): Lie down, I told you.

INES (Coloma): Do not waste your time, soldier. I will not do it. It is useless.

LAY SISTER 1 (Soldier): Come on, hurry up. The emperor awaits. You do not know what he is like when he is enraged. He is capable of anything.

INES (Coloma): While I live, you will not succeed. You will have to kill me first.

(*From the interior, the authoritative voice of the Emperor is heard.*)

ISABEL (Aurelius): Soldier! Soldier!

(*The SOLDIER becomes nervous, grabs the young woman by her arm and throws her on the floor.*)

LAY SISTER 1 (Soldier): I have told you to lie down. Do you not hear me? He will kill me! He will kill me!

INES (Coloma): Do not allow this, my Lord. Help me. I do not desire to offend thee. I do not desire to offend theeeeeee!

(*The screams of the young woman are mixed with a loud roar that emerges from below the platform. The SOLDIER is paralyzed with fear. An enormous bear appears. It takes the SOLDIER by the arm and pulls him away from the young woman. Then it lunges toward him and tries to strangle him.*)

LAY SISTER 1 (Soldier): Oh! Oh! Oh! Do not kill me. I am a simple centurion who just follows the orders of his emperor. I did not want to ... did not want to ... not want to harm her. Forgive me! Forgive me! I have a wife and two children in Rome ... I am not a bad person. Girl, do something. Tell it not to kill me. I promise to convert to Christianity ... I swear! I swear!

INES (Coloma): Set him free, good bear. The fright has been enough. This man arrived an enemy and he will leave as a brother.

(*The bear lets him go and then disappears the same way it entered. The SOLDIER kneels and kisses COLOMA's hands.*)

LAY SISTER 1 (Soldier): Thank you, girl! A thousand thanks! I will never be able to forget what you have done for me. You have saved my life.

INES (Coloma): You owe me nothing. Give thanks to God for showing your soul the light. Arise and tell the Emperor what your eyes have witnessed.

(The SOLDIER exits, walking backwards, sputtering and filled with joyous befuddlement. COLOMA moves downstage as she did at the beginning of the play.)

INES (Coloma): When Aurelius found out what happened, he was filled with rage. He ordered that they brutally whip me and tear out my flesh with iron claws. At last, it was a sword that felled my life. Upon arrival at my place of torture, I removed my shawl *(She takes it off.)* and I gave it to my executioners *(She flings it on the floor.)* and I chanted a prayer of supplication that melded with the sound of iron crossing my throat. From then on, I have been depicted as a virgin with a branch of white lilies and a white dove above my head.

(During her last few words, a dove descends to just above her head. Loud applause.)

(The doorkeeper's bell rings. The DOORKEEPER gets up and exits.)

JUANA: Did you enjoy it, Mother?

PRIORESS: Very much so, my children, very much so. Ines, come, let me give you a kiss. You were fantastic, sensitive and honest without losing any sweetness or love at any moment. Edifying, simply edifying! Who was the director?

MARIANA: Sister Catalina.

PRIORESS: Congratulations, Catalina. If our Lord had not called you, and the outside world did not prohibit this role to women, you would have been a great success in the world of theatre. Where did you get the bearskin?

MARIANA: It's not bearskin, Mother. It's from cats and rabbits, which we have sewn together and dyed.

PRIORESS: Such imagination! And, so much effort!

JUANA: A devout woman of Alba lent us the soldier's costume.

(*The DOORKEEPER enters running and looking nervous.*)

DOORKEEPER: Mother! Mother!

PRIORESS: What's the matter, my child?

DOORKEEPER: The Provincial! The Provincial! The Provincial has come!

PRIORESS: The Provincial? At this hour? And, without notifying us? (*The PRIORESS is scared, fearing the worst.*)

ISABEL: Don't be alarmed, Mother. He is probably just passing by on his way to Salamanca.

PRIORESS: God willing! (*To the DOORKEEPER.*) Distract him for a few moments while we tidy up. Come, my children, hurry. Take down the curtains, put the chairs back in their places, pull the table back from the wall. Just leave the platform where it is since there isn't enough time. Those in costume, disappear. Oh, goodness me, how nerve wracking. And it has to happen on my birthday of all days! (*She crosses herself.*) In the name of the Father, and of the Son, and the Holy Ghost. Amen. Oh, Lord, let Thy will be done.

(Jingling of keys. The DOORKEEPER gives a few knocks on the door.)

PRIORESS (*To the nuns*): All right, they're here now, go and just leave everything as is. (*They all exit through Door B. The PRIORESS runs to sit behind the table. She spruces up the veil of her habit.*) Come in.

(*The DOORKEEPER enters through Door C followed by the Provincial, BROTHER GREGORIO NACIANCENO and his companion BROTHER ANTONIO OF JESUS. The PRIORESS stands up.*)

DOORKEEPER (*Introducing*): His Reverence, the Provincial of the Discalced Carmelites, Brother Gregorio Nacianceno and Brother Antonio of Jesus.

(*The PRIORESS approaches to kiss the hand of the Provincial.*)

PRIORESS (*Insincere*): Very pleased to meet you. What a lovely surprise and so early, Brother Gregorio Nazarethan.

GREGORIO (Annoyed): Not Nazarethan, Nacianceno.

PRIORESS: I'm sorry. It sounds so similar. Congratulations on your new position. We've already received news of your election. So, are you just passing through?

GREGORIO: Well, not exactly. In part, yes, and . . . in part no.

PRIORESS: That's all right. You don't need to explain. It's to be expected when one is always so busy following God's eternal path. Have you had breakfast yet? May I offer you something?

GREGORIO: Thank you, Reverend Mother, but one of the principles that we are introducing into our mandate is that nuns desist with the smothering and spoiling of their provincials. Or, is it that you have not yet received the new norms?

PRIORESS: No, Your Reverence, but you've certainly given me advance notice with this reprimand. I was only planning to offer you a crust of stale bread and a little water.

GREGORIO: That's better. Austerity, hunger, and fasting! We need to end the luxury and squander! Gather together, gather together and pray! Punish the body, so that the soul may rise! You have all developed bad habits from the soft treatment of your former superiors.

PRIORESS: We've never been disposed to many delicacies at this convent. We've kept to lentils, eggs, bread, sardines, and once a week some type of meat.

GREGORIO: Oh, this convent has more than once offered a partridge or two to an illustrious visitor. More specifically, to my very own predecessor in this position.

PRIORESS: You do not lie, Your Reverence. But it was only out of courtesy that we offered it. If it bothers you so, don't worry, you'll only have an unsalted, half-raw sardine at lunchtime.

GREGORIO: I don't believe we'll still be here at that hour.

PRIORESS: What are you saying? Why are you in such a rush?

GREGORIO: I don't want to beat around the bush.

PRIORESS: So, then don't.

GREGORIO: We need to resolve this issue, for the good of everyone, as quickly as possible.

PRIORESS: You have me in suspense. What is it about?

GREGORIO: The body.

PRIORESS (*Playing dumb*): Ah, the whole body of the Holy Mother Church?

GREGORIO: Don't play dumb, Reverend Mother. You know exactly what body I'm talking about. I've come to take it.

PRIORESS: Take it? Where?

GREGORIO: To San Jose of Avila.

PRIORESS: Nonsense! Teresa died here, in Alba.

GREGORIO: While it is evident that did happen, she only died here by accident.

PRIORESS: Just exactly what are you insinuating?

GREGORIO: It's very simple. Brother Antonio of Jesus, here as a testimonial witness, will kindly explain everything to you. Please speak, Brother Antonio.

BROTHER ANTONIO (*Stammering*): Upon Mother Teresa's return from her founding in Burgos, I remained with her to accompany her to Avila. We arrived at a crossroads and I informed her that the Duchess of Alba was soon to give birth to a child and that she desired Mother Teresa's presence at the delivery. The Duchess was so devoted to Mother Teresa! Initially, the Reverend Mother resisted going to Alba. She informed me she was unable to travel there because she felt so very ill and wanted to return as soon as possible to the Convent of San Jose. Since I could not persuade her, and in my wretchedness did not realize the extent of her illness, and since so many had been the favors bestowed upon us by the noble House of Alba and in particular the Duchess herself for the Reforms, I ended up saying that it was actually an order. Then heading in the direction of Alba, Mother Teresa responded to that by saying: "I will go. But, I want you to know that this is the act of obedience that has cost me the most in my life."

GREGORIO: As you can see, Reverend Mother, it was not the will of God that brought her to Alba, but the will of the Duchess and an unfortunate order by a monk, who despite the fact that she was right in front of his nose, did not notice that even her spirit could not go on.

PRIORESS: That is all very well. But that proves nothing. No one can choose the date and location of one's own death. God alone has final say. No doubt there are reasons why it might make more sense to die in one place over another, but in the end, it is God, and only God, who determines this outcome. One might say that Brother Antonio was merely incidental in this event.

GREGORIO: You reason well for a woman, but it doesn't appear at all respectful to me that a nun, regardless of her position as prioress, dare refer to a monk as incidental.

PRIORESS: It was not my intention to offend you, it is just a manner of speaking. Your argument needed to be opposed with something all the more compelling.

GREGORIO: Well, anyway, there are other considerations, more along the lines of, let's say, the more humanistic and sentimental type. At the moment of death, as in one's old age, memories of one's childhood arise. One is intent on returning to the home and place of birth. It's a type of nostalgia that seeks to unify the poles of our existence. Mother Teresa was born for the Reforms at the Convent of San Jose in Avila. And that is why it was her desire to die there. An act of obedience impeded that. And, we, her sons and daughters, must, out of the grace of charity, gratify her in any way we can.

PRIORESS: I would be disposed to let her leave, were she still alive. I simply don't see the point of it now, since it's two years after her death, and she (as we would all agree) is already in heaven enjoying all the glories of paradise, Moreover, I am not certain that she would approve. Let me tell you an anecdote. I, too, am a witness and have testimonial. The day before she died, I went to her bed and asked her softly in her ear where she wanted to be buried. Do you know how she responded? That a dungheap would suffice, if we, here in Alba, were not willing to give her a little plot of earth. Believe me, she said it with such feeling and so very dismayed, it was evident that the question had really quite vexed her. Honestly, I do not think that the Reverend Mother Teresa would have put more feeling into one founding over all others. To her, we were all her daughters and all of the convents, her home. Her words, throughout the entirety of her life, completely reflected that sentiment.

BROTHER ANTONIO (*In GREGORIO's ear*): Where words don't work, maybe documents can.

GREGORIO: I can tell it's not going to be easy to convince you. I am going to be very clear. This affair has already been decided.

PRIORESS: Decided by whom?

GREGORIO: The Prelates of Pastrana!

PRIORESS: I have important connections—my husband was the Duke of Alba's accountant. And I am prepared to use them. I will move heaven and earth, if need be.

BROTHER ANTONIO (*Into the PROVINCIAL's ear*): Careful. Widows are the most dangerous. They come in already corrupted by the world. (*Spoken while the PRIORESS is in the process of talking.*)

GREGORIO: You won't be able to move anything. I have documentation—on two accounts. (*GREGORIO takes out a piece of paper from each pocket and holds them out.*)

PRIORESS: Care to explain yourself any better?

GREGORIO: Well, amen then to the humanistic and sentimental reasons which you so callously dismissed. In my right hand, I bear the Order issued by the Prelates, which prevents any obstacle to my departure, and, in my left hand, the signature of Mother Teresa, written with her very own hand, where she pledges with the Bishop of Valladolid to be buried next to him at the chapel in the Convent of San Jose of Avila [in exchange for defraying the costs of the works she had to do]. Religious power in one hand, civil in the other. I don't think your connections, no matter how well placed they might be, can override these.

PRIORESS (*Energetically*): With or without documents, she is not leaving here, because this is where God desired for her to die.

BROTHER ANTONIO: Don't get upset, Reverend Mother. What are important are her spirit and her doctrine. Why fight or get angry over a body?

PRIORESS (*Extremely angry*): Why? Because it is not fair for you to take her at this point! Why is it that you didn't claim her two years ago, when she died, when the knowledge of her incorrupt body wasn't known? Is it that sentimental reasons did not matter back then, nor had any of these documents been signed yet? You're not here to gratify Mother Teresa's wishes; you're here to steal the glory of her body.

GREGORIO: I cannot address that question. I am just given the orders, and you are to follow them.

PRIORESS: Those in charge should keep from ordering what they should not. Tear up the papers and let's be done with this.

GREGORIO: I will not permit such a tone! I should warn you that not only is your position as prioress in danger, but so is your habit.

PRIORESS: My position doesn't matter to me. It's at your disposal. I didn't come to the convent to give orders, but to obey. However, this is not an act of obedience, this is abuse and robbery.

GREGORIO: Quiet! Or I shall excommunicate you!

PRIORESS: No, not that! (*She flinches fearfully. Silence. Her resolve finally caves.*) You win. Here is the key to the tomb.

GREGORIO: That's better. Pray ten Our Fathers and one Apostles' Creed as penitence, then repent for your misconduct. May God forgive you.

BROTHER ANTONIO: This way, Reverend.

(*They both exit through Door B. The PRIORESS kneels, crying dejectedly. In the distance, a chorus of NUNS singing the morning prayers is heard. The number of singers begins to dwindle. There is an uproar. The voices of nuns are heard screaming.*)

VOICES: They're taking our Mother! They're taking our Mother!

(*The NUNS run hastily onstage followed by the two LAY SISTERS in the rear. They surround the PRIORESS. She gets up and throws herself weeping into CATALINA's arms.*)

ISABEL: Mother, we were in the choir and then suddenly—the smell. We expected the worst.

PRIORESS: That's exactly right, my children, and there is nothing we can do about it. They're taking her, or rather stealing her, more like it.

LAY SISTER 1: Reverend Mother, don't despair. We will not consent to this while there is still a drop of blood in our veins. (*She whistles.*) Sisters, sisters, all of you, to the door.

(*They all run and grab onto one another's arms tightly. They form a chain in front of Door C. GREGORIO and BROTHER ANTONIO appear through Door B. GREGORIO has a sack thrown over his shoulder and is followed by BROTHER ANTONIO. The PRIORESS who was waiting expectantly is standing about mid-stage. When she gets sight of them she lets out a scream of horror and almost faints. ISABEL steps over to catch her. She recovers almost instantly.*)

PRIORESS: Oh, such tremendous disrespect! Such heresy! Such sin! Our beloved Mother in a sack as if she were potatoes, acorns, or just animal feed! I do not want to see such a thing! I do not want to see how far the blind stubbornness of a provincial will go!

GREGORIO: The blind and stubborn one'll be you! And, if you previously had any influence in this world, the only thing you have now is obedience, the obedience that Mother Teresa most earnestly recommended that all nuns have for their superiors!

PRIORESS: Is it not ungodly, what my eyes perceive? Is it that you cannot even wait until we procure a casket for you?

GREGORIO: Out of the question. Any sort of casket would raise suspicions. The townspeople would be alerted and they would not let us leave.

PRIORESS: Where are you planning to take her right now? Oh, don't tell me, I can just imagine. You're taking her to an inn.

GREGORIO: Precisely. They're waiting for us at the hostel out front. We'll spend the day there and leave at nightfall. A sack and an inn won't rouse any suspicions.

PRIORESS (*Bursting into tears*): And, then you'll put her on the back of a mule as if she were a saddlebag! Isn't it a crime? Isn't it irreverent? Isn't it shameful for the body and for our Mother to flee like a criminal or a bandit, sheltered in the dark of night? Not even dead, will you allow her to rest from her travels!

ISABEL: Don't cry, Mother. There'll be no inn, no sack, no mule, and no saddlebag. From here she will not go.

(*All the NUNS echo ISABEL from the chain they have formed to block the door.*)

PRIORESS: Well said, my child.

GREGORIO (*In front of the door*): Clear the way.

ALL THE NUNS (*Moving in tighter on the door*): You won't be able to get through!

GREGORIO (*Handing the sack to BROTHER ANTONIO*): Obedience, discipline, constant observance! That's what's lacking here! (*Talking to BROTHER ANTONIO.*) A firm hand, a firm hand and authority! It's because of you and others like you, with your leniency, that a scene like this has been allowed to occur. We need to cut the wings of nuns, take away their freedoms, reform the constitutions. Mother Teresa, even if she was a saint, could not have imagined what would happen to nuns if permitted such latitude.

PRIORESS: What a contradiction! You want to take her body to exalt it, meanwhile you slaughter her doctrine and even aspire to change her Constitution. With all the hard work she went through to get it fully accepted. She checked every period and every comma!

GREGORIO: Be quiet and get out of here! That's an order!

PRIORESS: I will go, but I will not be silent. Soon, you shall see how my voice will be lifted up to the heavens. (*She exits through Door B.*)

GREGORIO (*Taking the sack back away from BROTHER ANTONIO*): Let's go! (*The NUNS still intertwined, now with their eyes shut, pray.*) Move away from the door! Hurry up! (*The NUNS do not budge.*) Is that so? We'll see about that! (*He puts down the sack again, takes out a crucifix from his pocket and brandishes it menacingly in front of the nuns.*) EXCOMMUNICATION! EXCOMMUNICATION!

(*All the NUNS let go, frightened; they disperse, clearing the door.*)

ALL THE NUNS: No, excommunication, nooooooooooo!

(*As the BROTHERS are about to cross through the doorway, the sound of the bells ringing desperately begins.*)

BROTHER ANTONIO: What is that? Why are the bells tolling?

GREGORIO: What do you think? The Prioress! (*To the NUNS.*) Halt those bells! (*INES and CATALINA leave running.*) Not only do all of you deserve excommunication, but also imprisonment. (*To BROTHER ANTONIO.*) If the townspeople come, we're in trouble. In the face of an angry mob, orders, authority, documents, and even excommunication don't matter.

(*The sounds of VOICES OF THE TOWNSPEOPLE now mix with the sound of the bells.*)

VOICES OF TOWNSPEOPLE: Open up, Sisters! The whole town is here to defend what's ours. They can't take her. She ours, ours, ooouuuurs!

GREGORIO (To BROTHER ANTONIO): Go look for the Prioress. Hurry up!

(*BROTHER ANTONIO runs through Door B. The voices from outside as well as the bells continue. The Provincial is speaking, but the noise drowns out his words. The bells desist. The screaming from outdoors continues. Enter the PRIORESS with BROTHER ANTONIO behind her.*)

GREGORIO (*To the PRIORESS*): Send that riffraff back to their homes immediately. May I remind you that I am the Provincial of the Order of the Discalced Carmelites. I have authority over this convent and I will have you excommunicated if you don't manage to make them go.

PRIORESS: How am I supposed to convince them of that at this point?

GREGORIO: Make up a lie, if need be! Tell them a sleepwalking nun grabbed the clapper of the bell! Whatever! Just make them leave!

PRIORESS: I'll see what I can do. May God forgive me. You have put me between a rock and a hard place, Your Reverence. Against the town, the convent, and myself, you force my obedience.

(*The PRIORESS heads towards Door C. At the threshold of the door, she turns back to the stage. The clamor continues.*)

GREGORIO: What's the matter? Why are you stopping? My threat is completely serious.

PRIORESS: I know, but I figure that this is a good time to negotiate.

GREGORIO: Speak! Quickly! What do you want in exchange?

PRIORESS: That you leave us a piece of our Mother as a consolation for the town of Alba and for this convent. An arm, for example. But, make it the right one.

GREGORIO: The right one, no. The left one.

PRIORESS: Then there's no deal! The left one's missing a hand.

GREGORIO: Fine, the right one, whichever. Just go immediately!

PRIORESS: Do you give your word?

GREGORIO: You have it. (*The NUNS display their pleasure. To BROTHER ANTONIO.*) Give me a knife.

(*The BROTHERS head toward the table and put the sack on it with their backs to the audience. The NUNS surround the table. The outside ruckus ceases. The PRIORESS reenters.*)

JUANA: How easy! It's like cutting a chicken breast.

(*GREGORIO wipes off sweat. He stops. He begins to wretch. He turns his head.*)

CATALINA: Or a piece of soft cheese.

MARIA: Blood is dripping. A little rag! A little rag to wipe it up!

(*INES gives her a handkerchief.*)

ISABEL: It has the texture of a leg of lamb.

(*MARIANA, wretches and moves away from the table and goes to a corner. The BROTHERS leave the arm and the knife on the table. GREGORIO puts the sack over his shoulder once again.*)

PRIORESS (*To the BROTHERS*): You may go now, if you wish. (*The BROTHERS don't respond and depart practically running. She holds Teresa's arm up high.*) My daughters, I promise you that I will not rest until that body, which now leaves, in hiding in the dark of night, returns to reunite with this arm in the broad daylight and with all the bells in the bell tower resounding through the air.

THE END

ABOUT THE TRANSLATOR

Karen Leahy was born in Puerto Rico. The daughter of a diplomat, she has lived in Latin America, Europe, Asia, and Australia. In addition to Spanish and English, she speaks fluent French and conversational German. She graduated with a BA from Smith College and has studied at the Université de Paris in France and the Dresdener Technishe Universität in Germany. She holds the masters degree in Spanish Translation from Rutgers-The State University where she taught intermediate Spanish and culture. Additionally, Karen Leahy has completed the two-year professional actor training program at the Maggie Flanigan Studio in New York City. Her other published work includes documentation of working conditions in the Free Trade Zones in Latin America. She currently works as a freelance translator and actor in New York City and resides in Jersey City, New Jersey.

TRANSLATOR'S ACKNOWLEDGEMENTS

My first and foremost thank you goes to Phyllis Zatlin for her generosity, insight, direction, and kind leadership as well as her editing, formatting, and other hard work in this process. May St. Teresa be with her. I am grateful to Concha Romero for writing such a lovely play, to Kerri Allen for her Note on the Play, and to Christine Jenack for her time and efforts. I would like to express gratitude for funding from the Program of Cultural Cooperation. Thank you also to Patricia Santoro for her early work on the play. I wish to thank the Catholic clergy members who were very important in this intellectual, but still rather spiritual endeavor, and who gave so much of their time and made every effort to instruct, explain, and enlighten me in the doctrines and practices of Catholicism. Most importantly among the clergy members I would like to thank Father Thomas Stanley for his way of understanding and his clarity and promptness in all of his responses. Very helpful and considerate, also, were Brother Don Neff and Padre Jaime (James Imhof). I appreciated the help and support of all my favorite Catholic laypeople who contributed to this project (Lawrence Leahy, Gladys Nieves, Margarita Leahy, John Donnelly, Michele Chang, Kathleen Leahy, as well as many others). Thank you to Maggie Flanigan, David Haugen, and my classmates at the Maggie Flanigan Studio for their theatre expertise as well as to my theatre and Spanish professors at Rutgers.

K.L.

CRITICAL REACTION TO THE PLAY

"*Un olor a ámbar* (*A Saintly Scent of Amber*) is a critical parody, tinted with black, grotesque humor and an absurdist tone that arises from the situations themselves, situations that in this case are based on a historical reality whose absurdity, cruelty and irreverence easily surpass fiction."

María Pilar Pérez Stansfield
Gestos (Irvine, CA), 1987

"Set in sixteenth-century Spain, Romero's *Un olor a ámbar* (*A Saintly Scent of Amber*) recreates the events surrounding the death of Saint Teresa of Avila (1515-1582) and the conflict over the possession of her mortal remains. While remaining faithful to historical documents, Romero combines contemporary dialogue and humor with the representation of past events, shedding light on the abuse of masculine authority and the silencing of the female voice."

Carolyn Harris
The Feminist Encyclopedia of Spanish Literature
(Westport, CT), 2002

"Noteworthy is Romero's capacity to elevate the image of Teresa's lifeless body to a heroic stature despite the covetous, self-serving, and manipulative efforts of the two towns to claim her corpse. Through a skillful use of language and dialogue, Romero recounts the historic event with an unmistakably modern air, a technique that has become her trademark."

John P. Gabriele
Spanish Women Writers. A Bio-Bibliographical Source Book.
(Westport, CT), 1993

"By emphasizing female creativity as a means of subversion in Arachne's representation of the rape of Europa and in the lay women's narration of the myth of Arachne, Concha Romero exposes her own creation, the drama *Un olor a ámbar* (*A Saintly Scent of Amber*), as a feminist revision —and thus subversion— of patriarchal history. Just as the characters' reinterpretations of traditional patriarchal narratives identify the female body as a site of oppression, Romero's revision of the debate over Santa Teresa's remains foregrounds the appropriation and subjugation of woman in patriarchial society."

Karen K. Sweetland
Entre actos: Diálogos sobre teatro español entre siglos
(University Park, PA), 1999

"Like the noblest writers of all times and places, [Romero] makes us ponder a fundamental theme: power in its various manifestations, political, social, religious and sexual. Here are reflected the threats of a dominant class that accuses of heresy or illness those who would function outside the order they maintain to perpetuate their dominance. If the rebels do not conform, they will be corrected (or liquidated) through the terrible threat of "excommunication" —real or symbolic— which can mean prison, exile, poverty, marginalization or death."

Patricia W. O'Connor
Preface to *Un olor a ámbar*, 1983

"*Un olor a ámbar* (*A Saintly Scent of Amber*) is above all a theatricalization of the Body: the incorruptible body of Saint Teresa, which one can feel, touch, finger, caress, and mutilate with morbid satisfaction; the body of the nuns, corseted in the discipline of this theatricalized convent but liberated by the language of the imaginary and of performance; and finally the body of the Church, splintered into various currents of thought and action, that reveals quite simply all too human traits."

Monique Martinez Thomas
Program notes for Les Anachroniques
Toulouse, France, 1996

"For the space of two hours, the action unfolded in a magnificent production. The actors held the attention of the spectators, moving them and making them feel the historical event that [Alba de Tormes] experienced when, after discovering the incorrupt body of the wandering saint, the Chapter of Pastrana agreed to transfer the body to the convent of San José in Ávila."

E. Sánchez
Tribuna de Salamanca, 2002

ESTRENO: CONTEMPORARY SPANISH PLAYS SERIES

No. 1   Jaime Salom: **Bonfire at Dawn** *(Una hoguera al amanecer)*
Translated by Phyllis Zatlin. 1992.   ISBN: 0-9631212-0-0

No. 2   José López Rubio: **In August We Play the Pyrenees** *(Celos del aire)*
Translated by Marion Peter Holt. 1992.   ISBN: 0-9631212-1-9

No. 3   Ramón del Valle-Inclán: **Savage Acts: Four Plays** *(Ligazón, La rosa de papel, La cabeza del Bautista, Sacrilegio)*
Translated by Robert Lima. 1993.   ISBN: 0-9631212-2-7

No. 4   Antonio Gala: **The Bells of Orleans** *(Los buenos días perdidos)*
Translated by Edward Borsoi. 1993.   ISBN: 0-9631212-3-5

No. 5   Antonio Buero-Vallejo: **The Music Window** *(Música cercana)*
Translated by Marion Peter Holt. 1994.   ISBN: 0-9631212-4-3

No. 6   Paloma Pedrero: **Parting Gestures** with **A Night in the Subway** *(El color de agosto, La noche dividida, Resguardo personal, Solos esta noche)*
Translated by Phyllis Zatlin. Revised ed. 1999.   ISBN: 1-888463-06-6

No. 7   Ana Diosdado: **Yours for the Asking** *(Usted también podrá disfrutar de ella)*
Translated by Patricia W. O'Connor. 1995.   ISBN: 0-9631212-6-X

No. 8   Manuel Martínez Mediero: **A Love Too Beautiful** *(Juana del amor hermoso)*
Translated by Hazel Cazorla. 1995.   ISBN: 0-9631212-7-8

No. 9   Alfonso Vallejo: **Train to Kiu** *(El cero transparente)*
Translated by H. Rick Hite. 1996.   ISBN: 0-9631212-8-6

No. 10   Alfonso Sastre: **The Abandoned Doll. Young Billy Tell.** *(Historia de una muñeca abandonada. El único hijo de William Tell).*
Translated by Carys Evans-Corrales. 1996.   ISBN: 1-888463-00-7

No. 11   Lauro Olmo and Pilar Enciso: **The Lion Calls a Meeting. The Lion Foiled. The Lion in Love.** *(Asamblea general. Los leones)*
Translated by Carys Evans-Corrales. 1997.   ISBN: 1-888463-01-5

No. 12 José Luis Alonso de Santos: **Hostages in the Barrio.** (*La estanquera de Vallecas*).
Translated by Phyllis Zatlin. 1997.
ISBN: 1-888463-02-3

No. 13 Fermín Cabal: **Passage.** (*Travesía*)
Translated by H. Rick Hite. 1998.
ISBN: 1-888463-03-1

No. 14 Antonio Buero-Vallejo: **The Sleep of Reason** (*El sueño de la razón*)
Translated by Marion Peter Holt. 1998.
ISBN: 1-888463-04-X

No. 15 Fernando Arrabal: **The Body-Builder's Book of Love** (*Breviario de amor de un halterófilo*)
Translated by Lorenzo Mans. 1999.
ISBN: 1-888463-05-8

No. 16 Luis Araújo: **Vanzetti**
Translated by Mary-Alice Lessing. 1999.
ISBN: 1-888463-08-2

No. 17 Josep M. Benet i Jornet: **Legacy** (*Testament*)
Translated by Janet DeCesaris. 2000.
ISBN: 1-888463-09-0

No. 18 Sebastián Junyent: **Packing up the Past** (*Hay que deshacer la casa*)
Translated by Ana Mengual. 2000.
ISBN: 1-888463-10-4

No. 19 Paloma Pedrero: **First Star & The Railing** *(Una estrella & El pasamanos)*
Translated by H. Rick Hite. 2001.
ISBN: 1-888463-11-2

No. 20 José María Rodríguez Méndez: **Autumn Flower** *(Flor de Otoño)*
Translated by Marion Peter Holt. 2001.
ISBN: 1-888463-12-0

No. 21 Juan Mayorga: **Love Letters to Stalin** *(Cartas de amor a Stalin)*
Translated by María E. Padilla. 2002.
ISBN: 1-888463-13-9

No. 22 Eduardo Galán & Javier Garcimartín: ***Inn Discretions*** *(La posada del Arenal)*
Translated by Leonardo Mazzara. 2002.
ISBN: 1-888463-14-7

No. 23 Beth Escudé i Gallès: ***Killing Time & Keeping in Touch*** *(El color del gos quan fuig & La lladre i la Sra Guix)*
Translated by Bethany M. Korp & Janet DeCesaris. 2003.
ISBN: 1-888463-15-5

No. 24 José Sanchis Sinisterra: ***The Siege of Leningrad*** *(El cerco de Leningrado)*
Translated by Mary-Alice Lessing. 2003.
ISBN: 1-888463-16-3

No. 25 Sergi Belbel: ***Blood*** *(La sang)*
Translated by Marion Peter Holt. 2004.
ISBN: 1-888463-17-1

No. 26 Cristina Fernández Cubas: ***Blood Sisters*** *(Hermanas de sangre)*
Translated by Karen Denise Dinicola. 2004.
ISBN: 1-888463-18-X

No. 27 Ignacio del Moral: ***Dark Man's Gaze and Other Plays*** (*La mirada del hombre oscuro. Papis. Osesnos*)
Translated by Jartu Gallashaw Toles. 2005.
ISBN: 1-888463-19-8

No. 28 Concha Romero: ***A Saintly Scent of Amber*** (*Un olor a ámbar*)
Translated by Karen Leahy. 2005.
ISBN: 1-888463-20-1
978-1-888463-20-0

ORDER INFORMATION

List price, nos. 1-11: $6; nos. 12-28 & rev. 6, $8.
Shipping and handling for one or two volumes, $1.25 each.
Free postage on orders of three or more volumes, within United States.
Special price for complete set of 28 volumes, $130.

Make checks payable to ESTRENO Plays and send to:

ESTRENO Plays, Dept. of Spanish & Portuguese
Rutgers, The State University of New Jersey
105 George St.
New Brunswick, NJ 08901-1414, USA

For information on discounts available to distributors and to college bookstores for textbook orders, and for estimates on postage outside the United States, contact:

E-mail: estrplay@rci.rutgers.edu
Phone: 1-732-932-9412 extension 25
FAX: 1-732-932-9837

NEW ADDRESS, EFFECTIVE 1 JANUARY 2006

ESTRENO Plays
Modern Languages Dept.–PNY
Pace University
41 Park Row
New York, NY 10038 USA

Phone: 1-212-346-1433
E-mail: ilamartinalens@pace.edu
sberardini@pace.edu

VISIT OUR WEBSITE:

www.rci.rutgers.edu/~estrplay/webpage.html

ESTRENO Plays is printed at Ag Press in Manhattan, Kansas.